Sophie's Lovely Locks

Written and illustrated by
Erica Pelton Villnave

Marshall Cavendish Children

The Author will donate a portion of proceeds from sales of the book to a hair donation program that benefits kids. For a list of places where you can donate your hair, please visit: www.ericavillnave.com

For Dad, who used to help me tame my lovely long locks   —E.P.V.

Text and illustrations copyright © 2011 by Erica Pelton Villnave

Marshall Cavendish Corporation
99 White Plains Road, Tarrytown, NY 10591
www.marshallcavendish.us/kids

LIBRARY OF CONGRESS CATALOGING-IN-PUBLICATION DATA
Villnave, Erica Pelton.
Sophie's lovely locks / by Erica Villnave. — 1st ed.
p. cm.
Summary: Sophie loves her long hair, but when it becomes too
hard to manage and she decides to get it cut, she finds something
generous to do with it. Includes list of organizations that make
wigs from donated hair.
ISBN 978-0-7614-5820-3
[1. Hair—Fiction.] I. Title.
PZ7.V733So 2011
[E]—dc22
2010010055

The illustrations were rendered in watercolor.

Book design by Vera Soki
Editor: Marilyn Brigham

Printed in Malaysia (T)
First edition
1 3 5 6 4 2

mc Marshall Cavendish
Children

My name is Sophie McPhee,

and I love my long hair.

Curly, curly, fancy, twirly.

Twirly, whirly, long, and girly.

Long hair is the best!

I love wearing my long locks
in braids with my flittery-glittery
butterfly ties or in pigtails with
my pretty pink princess clips.

I love how my hair *flies free* when I swing upside down, and how it *swirls* when I dance,

and how it *curls* when
I forget my umbrella.

But I don't love a snarly, tangly mess.

Oooch, eek, ouchy-ouch!

Maybe I shouldn't let my hair
be so curly, swirly, and twirly.

There must be something I can do

to keep my hair out of the way.

Sticky tape and goopy glue
should keep my hair up.

Sticky doesn't work.

Hmmm . . . what else can I do?

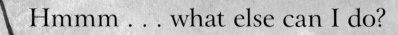

Pop!

Ooey-gooey,
super sticky.

Super sticky,
awfully messy!

How do I get this out?!

I need help!

Having long locks is too much work for me!

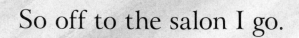

So off to the salon I go.

But what should
I do with all this
lovely long hair?

Give it to a mouse
for a warm home?

Give it to a bird for a nest?

I know! I'll donate it to
a girl who needs a wig.

Locks for kids
123

Donate
Your Hair
for Wigs

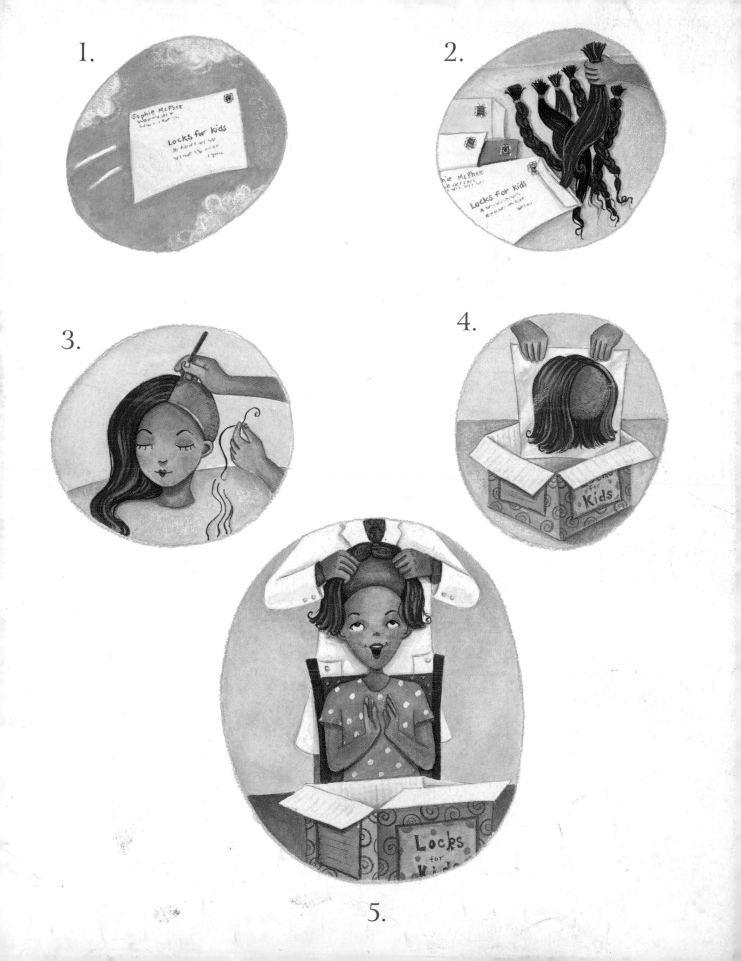

My name is Sophie McPhee,
and I love my locks . . .

. . . because two girls with short hair
are better than one girl with none!

Want to donate your own hair?
Check out these organizations.

Locks of Love
www.locksoflove.org

Locks of Love provides hairpieces to children ages eighteen years and younger in the United States and Canada suffering from any type of medical hair loss.

Pantene Beautiful Lengths
www.beautifullengths.com

Pantene Beautiful Lengths is a campaign that encourages people to grow, cut, and donate their hair to create free real-hair wigs for women who've lost their hair due to cancer.

Wigs for Kids
www.wigsforkids.org

Wigs for Kids provides custom-made hair replacements to children suffering from hair loss because of medical treatments, health conditions, or burn accidents.

Bouncy, bouncy, cute, and flippy.
Flippy, flippy, short, and pretty!

I love my new look!